Read all the Ninja Meerkats adventures!

NINJA MEERKATS

THE TOMB OF DOOM

GARETH P. JONES

SQUARE FISH

NEW YORK

COUNTY LIBRARY
TILLAMOOK, ORE.

SQUARE
FISH

An Imprint of Macmillan
175 Fifth Avenue
New York, NY 10010
mackids.com

NINJA MEERKATS: THE TOMB OF DOOM.
Text copyright © 2012 by Gareth P. Jones.
Illustrations copyright © 2012 by Artful Doodlers.
Cover illustration copyright © 2012 by Vince Verma.
All rights reserved. Printed in the United States of America by
R. R. Donnelley & Sons Company, Harrisonburg, Virginia.

The right of Gareth P. Jones and Artful Doodlers to be the author and illustrator
of this work respectively has been asserted by them in accordance with the
Copyright, Designs and Patents Act, 1988.

Square Fish books may be purchased for business or promotional use.
For information on bulk purchases, please contact the Macmillan Corporate
and Premium Sales Department at (800) 221-7945 x5442
or by e-mail at specialmarkets@macmillan.com.

Library of Congress Cataloging-in-Publication Data Available
ISBN 978-1-250-03402-1 (paperback) / ISBN 978-1-250-04598-0 (e-book)

Originally published in Great Britain by Stripes Publishing
First Square Fish Edition: 2013
Square Fish logo designed by Filomena Tuosto

10 9 8 7 6 5 4 3 2 1

For James and Nick (for the puns)
~ *G P J*

Gah! Not the fruit flies! What? Eh? Oh, I'm sorry, I was fast asleep and dreaming. What's that you say? Oh, do not worry— being a trained ninja, I would still have been able to protect myself while asleep. Sleep-fighting is one of the many skills you must learn to become a grandmaster. I once defeated an entire army of badgers in my pajamas! Now that I think about it, I never did learn how they got into my pajamas in the first place . . .

Now where were we? Ah, yes, I was about to introduce you to those brave and noble warriors, the Clan of the Scorpion: four fearless ninja meerkats, ever ready to defend the world from the villainous Ringmaster and his band of circus goons.

Just in case you're half asleep too, and need a quick reminder of their names, they are . . .

Jet Flashfeet: a super-fast ninja whose only fault is craving the glory he so richly deserves.

Bruce "the muscle" Willowhammer: the strongest of the gang, though in the brain race he lags somewhat behind.

Donnie Dragonjab: a brilliant mind, inventor, and master of gadgets.

Chuck Cobracrusher: his clear leadership has saved the others' skins more times than I care to remember.

Oh, and me, Grandmaster One-Eye: as old and wise as the sand dunes themselves.

This adventure takes place in Egypt, a country rich in history and mystery.

Oh, that rhymes! I'm a poet and I didn't even know it. Ha, that rhymes too!

Come to think of it, the great historian Trudy Ages was also an excellent rhymer. In fact, she wrote this short verse about Egypt.

The pharaohs of old
Were big fans of gold—
It gave them an excellent livin':
The problem with which
Was not them bein' rich,
But that when they died,
They took it all with 'em.

Now, let's get on with the story of . . .
THE TOMB OF DOOM.

CHAPTER ONE

A LOB DISTANCE CALL

It had been almost a month since the Clan of the Scorpion last encountered their deadly enemy the Ringmaster and his circus goons. They were enjoying a welcome break from saving the world back at their secret underground base in the Red Desert.

Or, at least, three of them were enjoying the break.

"I'm bored," moaned Jet, as he entered the main chamber of their burrow, trailing his nunchucks behind him.

"You could give me a hand with this,"

said Donnie, who was struggling with something flat, rectangular, and twice his size.

Bruce looked up from his bag of dry-roasted crickets. "What is that?" he asked.

"It's our new TV," said Donnie proudly, placing it on a table by the wall. "It's got a high-definition plasma screen and surround-sound speakers. Welcome to the future, my friends."

Chuck, who had been meditating silently in the corner, opened one eye. "Why do we need such a thing?" he asked. "We would only use it for keeping up with what is happening in the outside world, and we can already do that through the Internet."

"Ah, but it also has a webcam," said Donnie. "That means that once I've hooked it up, we'll be able to receive video calls on the big screen instead of on my smartphone!"

He pulled a remote control and some cables from his pocket, and connected the TV up to the power and the router.

"Hey, we could watch action films on it too!" Bruce pointed out. "Vin Pain has got a new movie out—it's called *Lethal Biscuit Two: Redunked*."

"Films are no substitute for the real thing," said Jet, spinning around and whacking a punchbag. "I'm *so bored*."

"You should be using this time for quiet meditation and practicing the art of kung fu, Jet," said Chuck. "Haven't you a new technique to work on?"

"Well, I *was* trying to learn one called the Squeeze of Rigidity," said Jet.

"That sounds cool," said Bruce. "What is it?"

"It's a move that causes your opponent's muscles to freeze, putting them out of action temporarily," Jet replied. "But my kung-fu manual went missing."

"You can borrow this one," said an elderly voice. "It is most entertaining."

Grandmaster One-Eye entered the chamber, clutching a book.

"Hey," exclaimed Jet. "That *is* my book!"

"Oh, is it?" asked the ancient meerkat. "Well, it's reminded me about some of the moves I used to do. When you get to my age, the jogging of one's memory is just about the only kind of jogging you can manage." He smiled and handed it to Jet.

"Did you ever perform the Squeeze of Rigidity, Grandmaster?" Jet asked.

"Oh yes, I was something of an expert at that one in my day."

"Would you demonstrate it for me?" asked Jet excitedly. "I've been practicing, but I can't work out how hard you need to—"

Grandmaster One-Eye reached out his paw and gently squeezed Jet's arm, cutting him short. Jet fell backward, his body completely rigid. Bruce jumped up and caught him just before he crashed to the floor.

"'ot 'id you 'o 'hat 'or?" mumbled Jet.

"Well, you did ask him to demonstrate the move," said Chuck with a wry smile. "And at least you're not bored anymore."

"No," Donnie laughed. "Now he's as *stiff* as a board."

Jet groaned. ·

"How long will he be like this for?" asked Bruce, laying him gently on the ground.

"Feeling will return to his body gradually over the next few hours," said One-Eye, looking quite pleased with himself.

"A 'ew 'ours?" Jet exclaimed.

"I believe the toes regain feeling first. He'll be as right as rain soon enough," the Grandmaster assured them. "The Squeeze of Rigidity, eh? Who would have thought I still had the knack!"

A ringing sound suddenly echoed around the burrow.

"What's that?" asked Bruce.

"An incoming call," said Donnie. "We can try out the new webcam!"

Donnie clicked the remote control and a single eye appeared on the enormous TV. The owner of the eye moved back to reveal a meerkat bearing a striking resemblance to Chuck, standing in a tunnel and wearing a sand-colored robe.

"It's my brother, Lob," said Chuck. "Lob, it has been too long! How is Cairo?"

"Greetings to you, Chuck," said Lob hurriedly. "I am afraid this is not a social call. I need your help."

"Grillian'!" said Jet.

"What did he say?" asked Lob.

"Don't ask," said Chuck. "What do you need help with?"

Lob checked over his shoulder, then whispered, "It is not safe for me to explain over a video call. Please come to Cairo and I will tell you everything."

"We will catch the next flight out," promised Chuck. "How will we find you when we get there?"

"Just tell me when you are due to arrive and I'll find you," said Lob. "Please hurry."

The screen went blank and Chuck turned to the others. "We have a mission."

"So, you're off to Egypt, eh? I once fought the Crazy Camels of Cairo there," said Grandmaster One-Eye with a wistful smile.

"Really? How did you defeat them?" asked Chuck.

"Oh, they were no match for my moves." One-Eye demonstrated with a karate chop that accidentally knocked over a row of fighting staffs. "Eventually they got the hump and ran off."

Donnie sniggered, but Chuck bowed respectfully. "You are indeed a worthy adversary, Grandmaster. But if you will excuse us, we must be on our way. Bruce, bring Jet. To the Meer-kart!"

CHAPTER TWO

THE ALLIANCE OF RIGHTEOUS RETURNERS

By the time the Clan reached the airport parking lot, Jet could wiggle his toes but he still had to be picked up and placed on a seat within Donnie's suitcase disguise.

"I've improved the design," Donnie explained. "Check it out."

Inside were four tiny bicycle seats, each with a set of pedals. Donnie sat at the front, behind the steering wheel. Chuck was behind him, followed by Bruce. Jet was at the back, and was just managing to cling on to the seat with his claws to keep upright.

"This is 'idiculous," he muttered.

"Right, let's get going," said Donnie. "Bruce, would you do the honors?"

Bruce pulled the suitcase closed, plunging them into darkness. "Hey, how are we supposed to know where we're going without eyeholes?" he asked.

"We don't need eyeholes," Donnie replied, pressing a button next to the steering wheel. A picture of the world outside appeared on a screen above it. "I've fixed a small camera on top of the suitcase, see?" He wiggled a joystick and the camera moved.

"Congratulations on yet another ingenious design, Donnie," said Chuck. "Let's head for Departures. We have a flight to catch."

By the time the plane touched down in Cairo, Jet had recovered full use of his limbs.

"Finally!" he said, bouncing up and down on his seat excitedly, as the suitcase moved around the luggage carousel.

"Keep still, Jet!" Donnie checked the screen. "OK, on the count of three, everyone lean to the right. One, two, three . . ."

If any of the other passengers had been looking, they would have seen one bag fall off the carousel and make its way toward the exit, moving alongside a tourist's suitcase to give the impression that it was an item of his luggage.

"Do you have any idea what kind of trouble Lob might be in, Chuck?" asked Jet.

Chuck shook his head. "I suspect that it will have something to do with his job, although he has never revealed what that is . . ."

The Clan passed through the Arrivals gate and out of the exit. The midday sun was high in the sky.

"Now, where is Lob?" asked Chuck.

"I am right here," said a voice.

Donnie twisted the camera around and saw a tatty brown suitcase in front of them.

"Follow me," said the suitcase.

The two bags made their way across the road and into some bushes, where Lob opened his case and climbed out. The Clan did the same.

"Nice disguise," said Donnie.

"It was designed by a rat named Rameses who, like you, Donnie, has a flair for invention," Lob said with a respectful bow.

"You know my name?"

"Your interest in gadgets suggests that you are the Clan's master inventor, Donnie Dragonjab," Lob replied. "Chuck speaks highly of you, as he does of all of the Clan."

"It is good to see you, Lob," Chuck said, bowing to his brother. "But what is wrong? Why have you summoned us?"

Lob looked around nervously. "Not here. I will tell you on the way into town."

"Which disguise do you want to use?" asked Donnie, delving into his rucksack. "I've got a sheep, a cow, a dog..."

"We do not need disguises in this city," said Lob. He reached down and lifted a trapdoor that revealed the entrance to an underground tunnel. "We'll take the tunnels. They were also built by Rameses, you know."

The meerkats followed him through the trapdoor and along a series of underground passages, high enough for them to stand upright and wide enough to walk side by side. Along the way, they passed several rats, cats, and mice. Each one greeted Lob with a salute as they passed.

"You are well respected here," said Chuck. "You must hold a position of great power."

"You are correct, brother. Apologies for my secrecy, but it was essential that I kept what I do under wraps," replied Lob. "I am commander of the Alliance of Righteous Returners—you will see how we operate shortly. We have a daily battle with the Thieves of Cairo. For many years the Thieves have relieved the city's tourists of their wallets and plundered this country of its treasures. The pharaohs were often buried with precious items, many of which were steeped in mystery and magic. The most dangerous of these objects has never been found. Like a fox hunted by a hound, it is safest while hidden, and we must help to keep it so."

Donnie smirked. "You'd never guess he was related to Chuck, would you?"

"So how can we help?" asked Chuck.

"Nuff's Head," said Lob.

"Enough said about what?" asked Bruce.

"No, Nuff's Head is the mystical object we need your help to protect. It is a golden mask once owned by the legendary Pharaoh Nuff, and is said to give the wearer the ability to see into anyone's mind."

"The possessor of such an item would acquire great power," said Chuck. "I can think of at least one man who would be interested in that... Where is the mask kept?"

"Within the Tomb of Doom," said Lob.

"Sounds lovely," Donnie replied.

"Once guarded by five magical Protectors, the entrance is located in the largest of the Queen's pyramids at Giza," Lob continued. "Legend tells of a door that only opens if a well-armed visitor touches the mummy's tummy..."

"Sounds simple enough," said Jet.

"But that's not all," replied Lob. "Inside, one must face the Junction of the Protectors where, it is said, every set of footsteps leads to death. Finally, one must choose which of the Triangular Doors to take. Many have tried to break into the Tomb of Doom, but few have survived to speak of its puzzles—and none have succeeded in deciphering them."

"I'm not surprised," interjected Bruce. "I didn't understand half of that."

"There is only one surviving Protector who knows how to solve the Tomb of Doom's riddles—an old owl by the name of Hootenkamun, or Hoots for short," Lob said. "His identity has been kept secret—until now. My spies tell me that the Thieves of Cairo intend to kidnap him and force him to tell them the tomb's secrets. My most trusted Returners have been watching over

Hoots, but we are not fighters. If we are to keep him safe, we need those accomplished in the art of combat. We need you."

"Of course we will help," said Chuck.

"Great," sighed Jet. "Sitting around protecting some old owl."

"Come on, it'll be a *hoot*," said Donnie.

"Tell me, Lob, why couldn't you say these things over the video call?" asked Chuck.

Lob lowered his voice again. "I believe there is a mole amongst the Returners."

"I haven't seen any moles," said Bruce. "I've seen cats, rats, mice . . ."

"He means someone working for the Thieves: a double agent," Donnie explained.

Lob led them up a steep tunnel, and out through a grate into a busy marketplace. Everything from silks and spices to souvenir sphinxes was for sale here. The exotic-smelling foods made Bruce drool.

"All this hustle and bustle makes it the perfect place for the Thieves to operate," said Lob. "We will be able to recognize them by the hooded cloaks they wear."

"But if they are so easy to identify, why have the police not dealt with them?" asked Chuck.

"The Thieves have friends in high places," Lob explained. "Official investigations into their activities never last long, and never result in arrests; it is only the Returners who stand up to them. Look, there's one now," he said, pointing at a man who was walking through the marketplace. He was wearing a dark blue cloak, the hood pulled low over his face, and had a monkey crouched on his shoulder. The man said something to the monkey; it climbed down, scampered over to an unsuspecting tourist, and removed his wallet from his pocket.

"He just stole that man's wallet!" exclaimed Donnie.

"Wait one moment," said Lob, as the monkey delivered the prize to his master, "and you will see the Returners at work."

A black cat slipped out from behind a nearby stall, snuck up on the Thief, and, with a precisely timed jump and an outstretched paw, swiped the stolen wallet from his cloak pocket. The cat carried it back to the tourist and returned it to his pocket.

By the time the Thief realized the wallet had been taken, the cat had vanished.

"Wow, that's one fast kitty," said Jet.

"I'm the quickest and the slickest, you won't hear me coming at ya. I'm the Thieves' worst nightmare and they call me Cleo Catra," said a voice behind them.

The meerkats turned to see a pair of green eyes peering at them.

CHAPTER THREE

A DATE WITH DESTINY

"Clan of the Scorpion, meet Cleo Catra. She is the best Returner we have," said Lob, introducing the black cat as she slunk out of the shadows. "Although she is supposed to be watching over Hootenkamun, not here dealing with street pickpockets," he added pointedly.

"Rameses is perfectly capable of guarding Hoots on his own for a few minutes. Besides, I wanted to meet this bunch of *mere*kats whose help you think we need," she sneered.

"Cleo, be nice," said Lob. "Please forgive her. We disagree about the best way to keep Cairo safe."

"My family has lived here for generations. We don't need help from outsiders, Commander Lob," Cleo continued. "You lot may be trained ninjas, but I learned my skills from the street, and you can't compete with my moves, so sweet."

"Oh yeah?" said Jet.

"Yeah," Cleo retorted.

"We don't have time for petty squabbling," said Lob. "Come on, we must get to Hoots."

Everyone followed him back down into

the tunnel. After a few more twists and
turns, the pathway led them inside a
building. A few moments later, they paused
in front of a grate, through which they
could see a room full of ancient Egyptian
artifacts, sarcophagi, and statues of strange
creatures and past pharaohs.

"We are inside the walls of the Egyptian
Museum," said Lob.

He led them up a miniature flight of stairs, at the top of which were some loose bricks in the wall. Lob removed them, and climbed through into a room full of dusty books, ancient-looking scrolls, crates, and boxes.

"The humans use this room for storage," explained Lob, weaving his way between piles of crates. "They rarely come up here, which is why I thought it would be a good place for Hoots to stay for a while."

The group rounded a corner and found themselves staring at a large stack of books. From the feathers scattered around, it was clear that this was Hoots's roost. But there was no owl to be seen.

"So where is he?" asked Donnie.

"Hootenkamun?" Cleo called, sounding slightly panicky. "Rameses?"

"Cleo?" replied a voice. "Is that you?" From behind a stack of boxes crawled a disheveled-looking rat. He scratched his head with his back foot, revealing a large pink bump.

"Rameses!" exclaimed Lob. "Are you all right?" The rat nodded, looking sheepish. "I'm sorry—

I didn't see a thing!" he said. "Someone knocked me out and took Hoots."

"It must have been the Thieves," said Chuck. "We'll go after them at once."

"A rescue mission," said Jet. "Now that's more like it!"

"Pah," said Cleo. "You can no more enter their headquarters without being noticed than a bear can sneak inside a beehive disguised in a yellow and black sweater."

"It's true," added Rameses. "It's impossible to infiltrate the Den of Thieves. We've tried."

"The Clan of the Scorpion doesn't believe in impossibilities," said Donnie.

"Very well," replied Lob. "But we must act quickly."

He led everyone back down into the tunnels. When they finally climbed out onto a narrow cobbled street in a deserted part of town, the sun was low in the sky. Lob, Cleo, Rameses, and the Clan hid in a shadowy doorway near the tunnel's exit.

"We are on the outskirts of town," said Lob. He pointed out a heavy wooden door set into a wall opposite. "And through there lies the Den of Thieves."

"Well, what are we waiting for?" asked Bruce. "Smashing in doors is what I do best."

"I admire your enthusiasm," said Lob. "But even if you were able to break that door down, you would be discovered immediately. The place is swarming with Thieves."

"There must be another way in," said Chuck.

Rameses shook his head. "There are no other entrances or windows, and no trapdoors. The stone floors make burrowing impossible. High, sloping walls and lookout turrets make going over out of the question.

The only way in or out is through that door."

"Then we'll go in disguise," said Donnie.

"You think we haven't tried that?" snapped Rameses. "They only let their own kind in. Watch. One is approaching now."

Just then, a Thief turned the corner. As soon as he reached the door, it opened. He slipped inside before the door slammed shut behind him.

"Intriguing," said Chuck.

"This is a waste of time," complained Cleo. "And the sound of the fat one chewing is getting on my nerves. Doesn't he ever stop eating?"

"Oh, sorry. D'you wanna date?" asked Bruce, speaking with his mouth full.

"A date? With you?" snorted Cleo. "Dream on."

"I meant do you want a date to eat?" he said, holding up a squishy black fruit.

"Where did you get that?" asked Donnie.

"There's a man around the corner selling them. I grabbed some when he wasn't looking."

"Hm." Chuck stroked his chin. "Bruce, show us this man."

Bruce led them back into the tunnel, and around the corner to another exit positioned opposite a stall. A bearded man sat on a stool behind the table laden with dates.

"I wonder how he makes any money in such a remote spot," said Donnie.

A Thief approached. He handed the man a coin and went on his way.

"Hey, he forgot his dates," said Bruce.

"Jet, get to that stall and see if anything strange happens when the next Thief comes along," ordered Chuck.

Jet nodded, then dashed across the road and ducked under the date-seller's table.

A few moments later, another hooded Thief arrived and handed the date-seller a coin. Shortly afterward, Jet reappeared.

"There's a button under the stall," he explained. "He presses it when the Thief goes around the corner."

"And that is what alerts those inside to open the door," said Chuck.

"So simple," said Lob.

"Yes, simplicity is the key," Chuck said thoughtfully. "Gather round, everyone— I have a plan."

CHAPTER FOUR

ENTER THE DEN

By the time the next Thief rounded the corner, the meerkats were ready for him. When Chuck gave the signal, Bruce leaped from the shadowy doorway and struck the Thief in the back of the knees. As he crumpled to the ground with a whimper, Jet delivered a double-fisted punch to the back of his head, knocking him unconscious. Bruce then dragged him over to the doorway, where Chuck and Donnie relieved him of his cloak.

Meanwhile, the date-seller was busy

trying to shoo Cleo away. "Scat!" he said. He hadn't needed to stock up on dates for several years and he wasn't going to be forced to do so now just because of some flea-ridden cat.

Cleo, however, was as fast as lightning

and extremely determined. She jumped
up onto the table, hissing and yowling, and
scattering dates everywhere. At that precise
moment, Lob slipped under the table
unnoticed, and waited for Rameses
to give him the signal to press the button.

The door to the Den of Thieves opened
and a short hooded figure stepped inside.
Hidden under the cloak were the meerkats:
Bruce was at the bottom of the stack, with
Jet standing on his shoulders; Donnie was
above him and Chuck was at the top, his
face hidden inside the cloak's hood.

The Clan of the Scorpion was standing
in a large stone courtyard, a single wooden
door in each of the four surrounding walls.
The place was packed with Thieves huddled
in small groups.

"How can we find out where the owl is
being kept without making ourselves too
obvious?" Chuck wondered.

"I've got something that might help,"
Donnie whispered. He reached into his bag
and pulled out a small gun-like device. "This
is a short-range sound amplifier." He flicked
a switch and passed it up to Chuck, who

pointed it through a sleeve of the cloak at a pair of Thieves. Suddenly they could hear the men as though they were standing next to them.

"Say what you like, I don't trust him. He's an outsider," said one.

"He did know about the owl, though," said the other.

"Hm. Well, as long as he comes good on his side of the bargain . . ." grunted the first man.

Just then two of the courtyard's doors creaked open. "Ah, here he is now," the second man said.

The Clan turned to see the Ringmaster's clowns, Grimsby and Sheffield, step from the right-hand door. Grimsby tripped over Sheffield's huge shoes and both clowns rolled over, then sprang back to their feet. Next, two men appeared from the left-hand door: one bare-chested and muscular, holding a burning torch, and the other short and skinny, and carrying a wicker basket.

A third door directly opposite the meerkats opened and a tall, shadowy figure wearing a top hat and carrying a whip stepped out. He was accompanied by a Thief carrying a cage with a black cloth draped over it.

"The Ringmaster," Chuck said through gritted teeth. "Of course."

"Gentlemen, I have bad news," he cried. "There is a thief amongst us."

The Thieves cheered and applauded, and the Ringmaster smirked.

"I can't see Doris," whispered Chuck, looking for the Ringmaster's faithful dog.

"Good Thieves of Cairo," continued the Ringmaster. "Allow me to introduce you to the last living Protector of the Tomb of Doom . . . Hootenkamun."

The Ringmaster pulled the cloth from the cage to reveal an extremely old and bewildered-looking owl.

"Thanks to your kidnapping skills," he continued, "we will soon control not just this city, but THE WORLD!"

The Thieves cheered.

"I'll never help you," the owl said in

a croaky voice. "My beak is sealed."

"Oh, really? Cat got your tongue, has it?" said the Ringmaster. "Doris!"

Doris the Dancing Dog appeared behind him, doing a backward tango and dragging a sack. The Ringmaster reached inside it . . . and pulled a black cat out by her tail. She yowled and struggled, trying to scratch her captor.

"They've got Cleo Catra!" Chuck gasped.

"Rameses must be the mole," Donnie whispered. "He's helped them catch Hootenkamun and now he's betrayed Cleo Catra too!"

"Your accusation is like a poorly built house, Donnie," Chuck warned. "It has no foundation."

"I know that cat," yelled a Thief in the crowd. "She's a Returner!"

"Indeed she is," the Ringmaster replied.

"Give her to us—we'll prove there's more than one way to skin a cat!" cried another.

The Ringmaster turned to the owl. "Perhaps I should throw her to the mob. What do you say, Hootenkamun? Are you willing to sacrifice the life of a Returner for some rusty old treasure?"

"Don't say a thing, Hoots!" cried Cleo.

"How very noble," said the Ringmaster, squeezing Cleo's tail. She hissed in distress.

"Don't hurt her!" begged the owl. "I will take you to the temple, but be warned—there are things there that are best left undisturbed . . ."

"I'll be the judge of that," the Ringmaster replied, shoving Cleo back into the sack.

"Don't forget your side of the bargain, Ringmaster," shouted one Thief.

"Yeah," yelled another, "you said you'd help us destroy the Returners if we brought you the bird."

"And so I will," said the Ringmaster. He held up a piece of paper. "This is a map of their underground tunnels, showing the location of every exit. You can get on with blocking them up while we visit the tomb. Then, with the help of my latest recruit, we will smoke the Returners out one by one. Gentlemen, allow me to introduce you to expert fire-eater . . . Bernie Lungs."

The bare-chested man with the burning torch thrust the flame into his mouth, then sent a burst of fire into the air.

The Thieves cheered and clapped.

"We must get word to the Returners to evacuate the tunnels," whispered Donnie.

"Quiet!" The Ringmaster cracked his whip, silencing the unruly crowd. "Only one thing stands in our way . . . Well, to be precise, four things standing on each other's shoulders. Thieves of Cairo, the Clan of the Scorpion has infiltrated your Den."

A concerned murmur swept across the courtyard as the Thieves glanced at each other suspiciously.

"The mole has struck again," muttered Chuck, keeping his head down.

"There is one way to find them," the Ringmaster continued. "Lower your hoods."

At first, the Thieves seemed reluctant to

reveal their faces but, one by one, they did
as they were told.

Eventually, there was just one hooded
figure left.

A smile spread slowly across the

Ringmaster's face. "And so the meerkats
are revealed. Welcome."

Chuck lowered the cloak's hood.

"Wherever you go," he said, his gaze fixed on the Ringmaster, "we will be one step ahead, ready to trip you up."

"Not this time," replied the Ringmaster. "Thieves of Cairo, take them!"

The Thieves put their hoods back up and drew their weapons.

"Time to fight?" said Jet.

"Time to fight," Chuck confirmed.

Chuck cast off the cloak, unsheathing his sword as he leaped off Donnie's shoulders. He made for the Ringmaster, but a hundred grasping hands stopped him from getting very far.

Donnie, Bruce, and Jet tried to leap to his aid, but the Thieves were everywhere. Within seconds, they had been separated.

Jet moved in a slow circle, spinning his nunchucks above his head, assessing his opponents. One Thief swung his long sword

THWACK!

at Jet, who jumped to avoid the attack, then used the blade of the sword as a springboard. He leaped at the Thief's face, landing a Full Palm Strike on his nose, and sending him reeling.

A second Thief came at him, wielding a mace. Jet dived out of the way, narrowly avoiding being flattened by the spiky weapon as it crashed to the ground. A third Thief stabbed at him with a knife from behind, but Jet swiftly ducked, then used a backward somersault to return to Bruce's side.

Bruce was keeping a circle of Thieves at bay, blocking their attacks, pelting them with his fists, and knocking others back with his tail, but there seemed to be an endless supply of the hooded villains.

Jet and Bruce bashed, kicked, and pummeled their way through the wall of Thieves until they found Donnie, fending off his aggressors with a staff.

"Donnie!" Jet cried.

Donnie swung around and accidentally caught Jet with the end of the weapon. It flashed with a blue electric spark and Jet shot into the air like a firework.

He quickly turned this to his advantage, performing a Hurricane Spin as he fell that caught a Thief on the chin, sending him sprawling.

"Sorry," said Donnie, zapping Thieves left and right. "I didn't see you there! You've heard of a pole vault? Well, this is a volt pole. It gives off a thousand-volt shock." He turned to look at Jet. "Woah! You should see your fur."

"Why? What's wrong with it?" The shock had caused Jet's fur to stand on end, making him look like a giant hedgehog. At that moment, a Thief came at them with a mallet and Bruce landed a heavy punch on his shins to save Jet from being flattened.

"Thanks," said Jet.

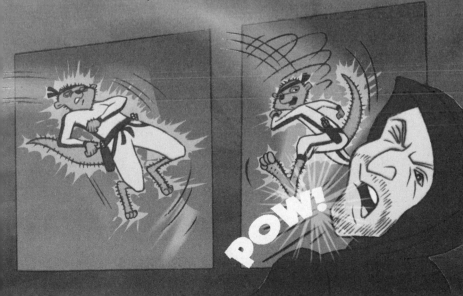

"We need to find Chuck," said Donnie.

"I've got an idea," said Jet. "When I jump up, use the stick on the soles of my feet, Donnie."

Donnie raised one eyebrow questioningly. "OK, if you say so!"

Jet sprang up over Donnie's head and Donnie jabbed him with the volt pole, sending him rocketing up above the throng. From his position, he could see Chuck battling ten Thieves on the opposite side of the courtyard.

"This way!" Jet cried as he landed, his fur smoking slightly.

The meerkats fought their way across the courtyard, and were reunited with Chuck just as he defeated the last of the ten Thieves.

"Glad to see you!" said Chuck. "The Ringmaster and his goons took Cleo and Hoots and went through that door."

He pointed to the wooden door in front of them. "We must follow."

"Bruce and I will handle this," said Donnie.

Donnie dived into the crowd, clearing a path to the door with the volt pole, zapping Thieves out of the way. The meerkats followed, and Bruce charged at the door with a cry of "Bruce Foooorce!" It smashed into pieces with an almighty crash.

The meerkats sprinted through the door and up a spiral staircase, the remaining Thieves close behind. At the top, Jet slammed the door, and Bruce barricaded it with some heavy crates he found nearby.

"What now?" asked Jet, smoothing down his fur.

They were standing on a turret at the top of a tower, and had a spectacular view of the pyramids at Giza, tinged red by the light of the setting sun. Sailing through the sky toward the magnificent structures was a black-and-red striped hot-air balloon.

CHAPTER FIVE

FANGS, SQUEEZE, AND MIRAGE

"Donnie," said Chuck, "can we use the Meer-kite to follow the Ringmaster's balloon?"

Donnie shook his head. "I haven't had a chance to repair it since Herr Flick shot us down in India." He pulled a harpoon-gun out of his bag. "We can use this to get to street level, then find a way to cross the desert quickly once we're on the ground."

"Lend me your binoculars, Donnie," said Chuck.

Donnie fished them out of his backpack and handed them to Chuck.

"OK," said Chuck, scanning the horizon. "Aim for that tree on the outskirts of the city. The one next to that drawing in the sand of a snake in the grip of a meerkat's paw. It's our family coat of arms—a message from Lob. He must be down there."

"Hey, I've got a coat of arms," said Bruce.

"No, Bruce, you've got a coat *with* arms," said Donnie. "That's not the same thing."

The Thieves were now pounding on the door, trying to break it down.

"Donnie, like actors in a film on fast-forward, we must act quickly," said Chuck.

Donnie took aim and fired the harpoon-gun. A metal hook flew high over the rooftops and latched on to the tree. He then cut the wire and tied it to the turret.

The meerkats grabbed the zip line and leaped from the roof just as the Thieves burst through the door.

"Wheeee!" Bruce cried, as the meerkats zoomed over the rooftops.

By the time the Thieves worked out where the meerkats had gone, the Clan had reached the ground. Donnie cut the zip line, preventing the Thieves from following, and retrieved the hook from the tree.

"A dramatic escape," said a voice nearby.

They turned to see Lob and Rameses step out from behind the tree.

"Lob, I am so glad you are all right," said Chuck. "When I saw they had Cleo Catra I feared the worst."

"After you entered the Den we remained to watch the door as you instructed," said Lob. "Cleo went to check on the date-seller, and they must have got her then. Not long after, we saw a black-and-red hot-air balloon launch from the top of the tower."

"That was the Ringmaster," said Chuck.

"Why didn't you follow him?" asked Jet.

"Our desert buggy has broken down," said Lob, gesturing toward what appeared to be a child's replica dune buggy. A toolbox was on the ground nearby. "Rameses has been repairing it."

"I'm sure he has . . . not," said Donnie.

"What's that supposed to mean?" asked Rameses.

"Oh, come on!" exclaimed Donnie. "It's obvious that you're the mole."

"I thought he was a rat," said Bruce.

"Well, he certainly *ratted us out*," said Donnie. "He delivered Hootenkamun to the Thieves, he helped catnap Cleo, and he told the Ringmaster we had infiltrated the Den."

"You have no evidence of that!" Rameses cried.

"Indeed," Lob agreed. "Rameses is one of my most trusted Returners. Remember, it was he who designed the tunnels."

"Meaning he could supply the Ringmaster with a map of all the exits," said Donnie.

"The Thieves have a map of our tunnels?" said Lob, sounding panicked.

"Yes, and they are planning to block up the exits and smoke everyone out," said Chuck. "You and Rameses must alert the other Returners and evacuate the tunnels immediately. We will follow the Ringmaster to the Tomb of Doom."

"Very well," said Lob. "But be warned—the tomb contains much danger."

"Don't you worry about us, we can look after ourselves. You just make sure you keep an eye on that rat," said Donnie.

Rameses snarled, then turned and followed Lob back toward the city.

"Can you fix the buggy, Donnie?" asked Chuck.

"Was my mother a meerkat?" Donnie replied.

"You don't know if your mother was a meerkat?" said Bruce.

"I was being . . . oh, never mind." Donnie jumped onto the buggy and whizzed around tightening screws, twisting knobs, and hammering. After a couple of minutes, he turned the key and the engine started.

The meerkats hopped in and sped into the desert as the sun set.

By the time they arrived at the pyramids the only light was from the moon and stars, and the colored floodlighting that highlighted the magnificent structures.

Donnie drove past the Sphinx and around three large pyramids. At the foot of one of the smaller pyramids, the meerkats spotted a distinctive black-and-red hot-air balloon. Getting nearer, they spied two wicker baskets at its base.

"It would appear that the Ringmaster left something behind," said Chuck.

"His laundry by the looks of it," said Donnie.

He turned off the engine and the meerkats approached on foot. Suddenly the lid of one of the baskets flew off and the skinny man from the courtyard hopped out.

"I'll deal with this wimp," said Jet.

"With your kung-fu skills, I am sure you

could knock me out in a second, Jet Flashfeet," said the man, "but let's see how you deal with this blow." He pulled out a flute and played a short tune.

Three snakes slithered out from under the lid of the other basket—a huge boa constrictor, a cobra, and a sidewinder.

"I am Juan Spitten—the world's greatest snake charmer," said the man. "And these are my *charming* companions: Fangs, Squeeze, and Mirage."

"My family name is Cobracrusher for good reason," said Chuck, drawing his sword as one of the snakes moved toward him, raising its head threateningly.

"Fangs here is loaded with enough poison to end your little life," Juan said.

Fangs lunged at Chuck, but he rolled out of the way just in time. The other two snakes were hot on his tail, though. One tripped Chuck up, while the other wrapped itself around him, squeezing so hard that his sword fell from his hand.

"You'll have to forgive Squeeze—he's a bit over-friendly," laughed the snake charmer.

Just as Bruce and Donnie sprang to Chuck's aid, the sidewinder whipped up a cloud of sand with its body, making it impossible to see more than a few centimeters in front of them. Snake-like shapes appeared within the cloud.

"Where is he?" cried Bruce.

"This must be Mirage's work. He's trying to confuse us," said Donnie. "My Instant Wind Maker will put an end to that." He pulled what looked like a leaf blower from his backpack and began to disperse the sand, but neither he nor Bruce realized that they had backed toward Squeeze.

"Behind you!" Chuck cried weakly.

But it was too late. Still keeping hold of Chuck, Squeeze lifted his enormous tail and wrapped it around Donnie and Bruce.

Fangs and Mirage advanced on Jet. Fangs's fangs glistened in the moonlight, and Mirage's body shifted menacingly through the sand.

"Now I will succeed where all others have failed and destroy the Clan of the Scorpion," proclaimed Juan. "You are defeated, admit it!"

"We're Ninja Meerkats," said Jet. "The only *defeat* we know are *de ones* on *de end* of *de legs*."

Juan smirked. "Fangs, Mirage—finish him!"

Bruce, Donnie, and Chuck watched helplessly as Mirage whipped up a thick sand cloud. Jet and the two deadly snakes vanished from sight.

When the sand settled, it took them a moment to figure out what they were looking at. Mirage lay on the sand, his body tied in a neat bow, and Jet appeared to be holding a long stick . . . which was, in fact, Fangs. The snake was as rigid as a tree branch, frozen with its jaws wide open.

Chuck smiled. "The Squeeze of Rigidity."

"Oh yes!" Jet nodded. "Now, let's see how deadly this poison really is."

He swung Fangs at Squeeze, sinking the frozen cobra's teeth into the boa constrictor's body.

Squeeze hissed and recoiled instantly, releasing Chuck, Bruce, and Donnie.

Chuck picked up his sword and held it to Juan Spitten's throat.

"Now, Juan, where is the Ringmaster?" he demanded.

"In th-th-there," he stammered, pointing to the nearest small pyramid.

"How do we get in?"

But before Juan could answer, Mirage freed himself and whisked up another cloud of sand. By the time Donnie had cleared the air with his Instant Wind Maker, the snake charmer had disappeared, along with Squeeze and Mirage.

"Shall we go after them?" asked Bruce.

"No," said Chuck. "There is no time. We must follow the Ringmaster and save Hoots."

"What about him?" asked Jet, holding up Fangs.

"Perhaps he has learned that crime doesn't pay," said Chuck.

"Yeah," said Donnie. "I think he'll *go straight* from now on."

"Come, we must hurry," said Chuck. "The Tomb of Doom awaits."

CHAPTER SIX

INTO THE TOMB

"Hmm," said Chuck, pondering the strange symbols and hieroglyphs that covered the blocks of stone at the base of the pyramid. The largest image was a picture of a mummy with holes in different parts of its body. "My brother spoke of a well-armed visitor needing to touch a mummy's tummy in order to enter. Donnie, what do you make of these holes in the rock?"

"Well, they're more like slits than holes. And look, there are scratch marks around the edges of each slit," Donnie stated.

"That's it!" Chuck drew his sword. "I must thrust my sword into the hole where I would expect to find the mummy's tummy."

"So, the hole in its middle," said Jet.

"I think not," said Chuck. "In ancient Egypt the internal organs were removed during mummification. Look closer. What do you see drawn by the mummy's feet?"

"It's a jar," said Bruce.

"A canopic jar, to be precise . . . containing the mummy's stomach."

Chuck thrust his sword into the slit at the center of the jar.

Suddenly there was a rumble, and the stone block slid back, revealing the entrance to a tunnel.

"So the door was *a jar* all along," said Donnie, chuckling.

"I don't get it," said Bruce.

As they entered the pyramid, Donnie pulled a flashlight out of his backpack to light their way. The path sloped downward, and the tunnel's walls were covered with engravings depicting great wars, majestic hunts, and strange mythical creatures. The Clan stopped when they reached a junction made up of five paths.

"Which way do we go?" asked Jet.

Donnie shone his torch on the arches above each pathway, revealing drawings of a cat, an owl, a bull, a horse, and a jackal.

"This must be the Junction of the Protectors," said Chuck.

"And look—footprints," said Bruce, pointing at the ground.

Set into the stone floor were five sets of footprints, one leading into each of the tunnels.

"Lob said that all five sets led to death," recalled Jet.

"So none of these paths is the right one?" said Bruce, scratching his head.

"To follow in the *footsteps* of any of these animals would mean death," said Chuck. "But one of these animals can choose *not* to leave footsteps."

"The bird," said Donnie.

"Exactly."

"Great," said Jet, starting off in that direction. "Then we're going this way."

"Wait—listen." He picked up a small rock and threw it into the corridor. They waited to hear it land, but no sound came. "There *is* no path," said Chuck. "The bird's footsteps will also lead to a sticky end."

"So, what? We're supposed to fly, are we?" asked Bruce.

"Exactly," said Chuck.

"No problem," said Donnie. "Jet, hold my flashlight." He pulled the harpoon-gun from his backpack, and fired it at the roof of the corridor featuring the bird's footprints.

He checked that it was secure, then said, "Now hang on."

The others clung on to the cable and jumped. They swung into the darkness, over a huge hole, and landed safely on the other side. Donnie cut the cable and stuffed the harpoon-gun back in his backpack.

They were now in a second, much wider corridor, its walls lined with doors.

"The Triangular Doors," said Chuck.

"But they aren't triangular," said Bruce.

"No, but there are triangles *on* the doors," said Jet, pointing out how each door had a different number of triangles carved on it.

"Only one of these doors is the right way," said Chuck. "The others will—"

"Let me guess," interrupted Donnie. "Lead to certain death?"

"Exactly."

"What's this?" asked Donnie, pointing

at some carvings in the ground nearby. "A door, an eye, and a large triangle with some smaller ones inside it."

"I think it means the door we need to take has the same number of triangles carved into it as seen here," said Chuck.

"Well, that's easy," said Bruce, counting the triangles. "There are nine of them."

"No, there are ten," said Donnie. "The nine smaller triangles make up a big one."

"The answer is thirteen," said Chuck. "Look again. Within the big triangle are three medium triangles, each made up of four small triangles. We must take the door with thirteen triangles on it."

When they found the correct door, Bruce pushed it open, and the meerkats cautiously stepped inside. Suddenly, the ground fell away and they slid down a chute, landing with a THUMP inside a wire cage.

"Looks like thirteen wasn't the right

answer after all," Jet observed.

"Yes, it was," Chuck replied, "but it would seem our old enemy has beaten us to it."

They were suspended above a deep well at the center of a room filled with treasure. Five magnificently decorated sarcophagi stood at regular intervals around the walls, and at the edge of the well were the clowns, Doris the Dancing Dog, and Bernie Lungs. Hootenkamun was behind them, a chain around his neck tying him to a table leg.

"How nice of you to *drop* in," boomed the Ringmaster's voice from a shadowy doorway at one end of the chamber. "What a shame you can't hang around," he chuckled, "but it seems you're due to meet your doom . . . in the Bottomless Pit."

"I think not, Ringmaster. This tomb will be your own doom," said Chuck.

The Ringmaster stepped out of the shadows to reveal that he was wearing a gold mask.

Chuck gasped.

"Yes, Chuck, this is indeed Nuff's Head. And no, you won't be getting the better of me this time. As we speak, Jet is considering using a Butterfly Punch on the bars to release you." The Ringmaster cracked his whip on the cage, knocking the meerkats off their feet. "Donnie is reaching for his grappling hook, unaware that if he pulls it out, Bernie will turn you furballs into four little *fire*balls. And you, Chuck, you are thinking about all the ways you will attack me once you are free."

"Hey, he's reading our thoughts!" exclaimed Bruce.

"Precisely," said the Ringmaster. "How do you think I was able to ensnare you? I've been monitoring your progress by reading your thoughts since you entered this pyramid. In the past you've only managed to get the better of me because you had the element of surprise on your side, but there will be no surprises today. Now, before we bid you farewell, perhaps you'd like to say hello to my new friend."

Cleo Catra stepped out from behind a pile of treasure and weaved between the Ringmaster's legs. Doris eyed her warily.

"So it was you who betrayed the Alliance," said Jet.

"Of course," she purred. "My family was once worshipped as royalty in Egypt, and with the Ringmaster's help, that can be true again. I am Cleo Catra, here to make a scene; soon you'll all bow down to me as queen!"

"Indeed," said the Ringmaster. "Rest assured, I'll know of any attempt you make to escape before you even move. Yes, Donnie, that includes your smoke-grenade idea; and no, Jet, I don't think even you could pull off a move like the one you're contemplating. But please, do give it a try."

"You will live to regret this, Ringmaster," warned Hootenkamun. "Nuff's Head should not be used for evil."

The Ringmaster's laughter echoed around the tomb. "Somehow, I knew you'd say that," he smirked. "Now, Bernie, send them down."

Bernie Lungs took a deep breath and lifted his torch to his mouth. He exhaled, sending a huge flame at the rope the cage was suspended from, setting it alight. Doris barked happily, and the clowns applauded.

Suddenly, Bruce burst through the cage door. He flung himself at the Ringmaster, landing a powerful punch on his chest. "Bruce Force!" he yelled.

WHAM!

The Ringmaster staggered backward.

Chuck, Donnie, and Jet jumped to safety the moment before the cage dropped into the hole.

"But . . . I should have known he was going to do that!" the Ringmaster cried furiously.

"The wearer of Nuff's Head can read anyone's thoughts," said Hootenkamun. "But it is of no use against those ruled by instinct."

"I'm more of a doer than a thinker," said Bruce, as he cracked his knuckles.

Chuck drew his sword and turned to the Ringmaster. "So can you tell what I am thinking now?" he asked.

"Oh, how very predictable," sighed the Ringmaster. "You are thinking that before you, each enemy cowers, for now you'll fight till victory is yours. But I'm afraid you have not taken into account some of my latest recruits."

"Ha! We saw off your snake charmer," said Jet, "and we'll put out your fire-eater too."

"Oh, I'm not talking about Bernie," said the Ringmaster.

Slowly the doors to the five sarcophagi opened and from each one stepped a groaning, moaning mummy.

CHAPTER SEVEN

THE MUMMIES OF NUFF

The Clan of the Scorpion watched in horror as the five mummified figures slowly approached.

"Mummies of Nuff," said the Ringmaster, "these meerkats have broken into the temple to steal its treasures. Get them!"

The mummies turned their featureless faces toward the meerkats.

"Hey, Grimsby," said Sheffield. "You forgot to get a card."

"What for?" asked Grimsby.

"*Mummy's* day," Sheffield chuckled.

Chuck addressed the mummies. "It is not us who seek to steal the treasure," he said.

"It's no use," cried Hootenkamun. "They only hear the thoughts of he who wears the mask."

"Yeah? Well, these guys will need a whole lot more bandaging when I'm through with them," said Jet. "It's time for some Ninja-Tomb-of-Doom-boom!"

He grabbed hold of a loose bandage on one of the mummies' outstretched arms and swung from it, landing a powerful kick on its stomach. But instead of knocking it over, Jet flew straight through its belly and came out the other side, covered in bandages.

The mummy looked down at the hole Jet had made, and grabbed him.

"Hey, he went through the mummy's tummy," chortled Grimsby.

"What a dummy," added Sheffield.

"It's time to wrap up this situation," said Donnie. He ducked an attack from one mummy, then grabbed a loose end of bandage and pulled as hard as he could.

WHOOOSH!

The mummy spun around, but when it recovered its footing, it groaned angrily and swiped at Donnie. The meerkat rolled out of the way, then leaped to his feet.

"So," said the Ringmaster. "It appears the Clan of the Scorpion will meet their doom at the hands of a few old mummies. How sad."

Chuck turned to face him.

"Yes, Chuck," said the Ringmaster patiently. "I know you want to retrieve the mask so the mummies will be on your side, but there's nothing you can do to surprise me. Luckily, *we* can still surprise *you*."

A sudden burst of fire shot down at Chuck from the mouth of Bernie Lungs. He jumped out of the way, but not before the fire singed the end of his tail. Doris barked happily.

"Hey, Grimsby," said Sheffield. "I think Chuck's *burned* out."

"I tell you what, Chuck," said the Ringmaster, "I'll give you and your Clan a chance. Come and work for me and I will call off the mummies. After all, each member of the Clan has special talents. I'm sure we could find places for you in the circus."

"You can't trust the meerkat," hissed Cleo Catra. "He would double-cross you."

"Don't worry, my dear. I am wearing Nuff's Head," said the Ringmaster. "I will know if he is telling the truth."

"We'd never join you," said Chuck. "The Way of the Scorpion teaches of honor and honesty—things you will never understand."

"No matter," the Ringmaster replied. "I shall rule the world with or without your help. Now that I have Nuff's Head, I can read every thought—just imagine how powerful I'll be! Soon the world will be a giant circus and I, its Ringmaster!"

Suddenly, there was a loud rumbling from deep underground. The tomb shook, and chunks of rock tumbled from the ceiling.

The mummies immediately stopped
fighting, and the one holding Jet released
him. All of them raised their hands to their
heads and moaned, "Toooooomb!
Doooooom!" over and over.

"What are you doing?" bellowed the
Ringmaster. "I ordered you to destroy them!"

CRASH!

"The mummies hear *your* thoughts too, and their minds are linked to the tomb," Hoots said. "Now that they know your plan, the tomb is collapsing. I warned you that Nuff's Head cannot be used for evil."

While their enemy was distracted by Hoots's words, Bruce ran at him, knocking the Ringmaster to the ground. Jet prized the mask from the Ringmaster's face.

"So, can you tell what I'm thinking now?" asked Jet.

Before the Ringmaster could answer, Cleo Catra leaped up and pounced on Jet. The two of them rolled around on the ground, a struggling ball of fur. Cleo bit Jet's arm and he cried out, releasing Nuff's Head.

Doris bounded across the room, dodging falling rocks, and dived at the mask, but Chuck beat her to it.

"Nuff's Head fits anyone who dares to

wear it," Hootenkamun shouted out.

Chuck held the mask to his face.
It suddenly shrank, fitting him perfectly.

"Are you thinking what I'm thinking,
Sheffield?" asked Grimsby.

"Yes, he is," Chuck observed.

The clowns made for the door.

Meanwhile, Cleo Catra and Jet were
standing whisker to whisker near the edge
of the Bottomless Pit.

"Come on, we can settle this once we've
got out of here," said Jet.

"No way," spat the cat, swiping at him
with her claws.

Jet delivered a kick that sent Cleo flying
backward. She screeched and jumped up,
launching herself at Jet, but the meerkat
ducked out of the way and Cleo flew into
the Bottomless Pit. Jet grabbed her tail
just in time.

"Stop wriggling!" he yelled.

"Bruce, help Jet with Cleo," said Chuck.

Bruce hurried over, and together he and Jet pulled Cleo out of the pit.

Chuck turned to see the Ringmaster, Bernie, and Doris hurriedly following the clowns out of the tomb. A huge lump of stone fell behind them, cutting off their exit.

Chuck looked into Donnie's mind. He was pondering which of his gadgets was most useful. "The retractable grappling hook should do it," Chuck agreed.

Donnie delved into his backpack and pulled out the grappling hook and its controller. He fired the hook back up the chute. "Everyone grab on!"

"Can you read my thoughts as well, young meerkat?" Hootenkamun asked.

Chuck smiled at the owl. "You think there is no need to save an old bird like you, and that I should leave you and the mask here so neither of you will ever be found."

"Just so," said Hoots.

"I am sorry, I can fulfill only one of your wishes," said Chuck. He pulled Nuff's Head off and tossed it into the Bottomless Pit. Then he drew his sword and sliced through the chain binding Hootenkamun to the table. "We leave no one behind."

He put his arm around Hootenkamun and grabbed on to the rope. Bruce held on too.

Jet wrapped one arm around Cleo's middle and grabbed the rope with his other paw.

"You saved me," said Cleo.

"Not yet, I haven't."

"Let's go," said Donnie. He pressed a button on the controller and they shot up and out of the collapsing tomb.

CHAPTER EIGHT

A FINAL THOUGHT

The next morning, Lob led the others through the tunnels back to the bushes across the road from the airport.

"Well, brother," said Lob. "You have saved the day. The Alliance of Righteous Returners are unscathed, and Nuff's Head will never be found now that the tomb beneath the pyramid has collapsed."

Chuck nodded. "Yes, and that means Hoots is free to live the rest of his life in peace. I am pleased we could help."

"What of the map detailing the exit

points of your tunnels?" asked Donnie. "How will you continue to operate?"

"I have already begun work on new tunnels," said Rameses.

Donnie looked sheepishly at Rameses. "I owe you an apology," he said.

"Think nothing of it," said Rameses. "After all, none of us suspected Cleo."

"I betrayed your trust," said a familiar voice behind them. "And for that I am sorry."

They turned to see Cleo creeping out of the tunnel.

"Why, you traitor . . ." snarled Rameses.

"What are you doing here?" asked Lob.

It was Chuck who answered. "She is to board the plane with us," he said.

"I saw I had made the wrong choice the moment that the Ringmaster left me to die," said Cleo. "I will find somewhere to start a new life."

"It is with regret that I bid you farewell, Cleo, but your decision is the right one," said Lob. "But what of the Ringmaster himself? There has been no sign of him or his troupe since they left the pyramid."

"We will catch up with them soon enough, no doubt," said Chuck. "I am just pleased that we stopped him from stealing the mask—an enemy that can read your thoughts is formidible indeed. That said,

I was sad to part with Nuff's Head." A slow smile spread across Chuck's face. "Being able to see into your minds was most enlightening."

"What did you learn about us when you were wearing it?" asked Donnie.

"Well, in Jet's thoughts I saw great determination and honor as he fought for Cleo Catra's life. In yours, Donnie, I witnessed the workings of an amazingly resourceful mind."

"What about mine?" asked Bruce.

Chuck placed a hand on Bruce's shoulder. "It was your ability to act without thinking that saved us from an endless fall into the Bottomless Pit," said Chuck. "And yet while the rest of us were contemplating the very real possibility of our own deaths, you were wondering what you would have for dinner when you got home."

Bruce smiled and licked his lips. "Garlic grasshoppers and red onions."

Chuck laughed. "Well, you've definitely earned it. Come, Clan of the Scorpion—back to our burrow!"

In the meerkats' sixth adventure, the mystical stone of life has fallen into the wrong hands and an army of statues is causing chaos on the streets of London! Can the meerkats save the city before it's too late?

Find out in

**Ninja Meerkats:
Big City Bust-Up**

CHAPTER ONE

LONDON CALLING

In the early evening hustle and bustle of Covent Garden no one paid any attention to the automatic street-cleaning machine that trundled over the cobbles, whisking up discarded trash with its two spinning brushes. Certainly, no one suspected that inside the machine were four Ninja Meerkats.

Donnie was sitting at the front, using a control that he had installed to override the automatic route of the cleaner. He steered the machine around the tourists, market stalls, and street performers that filled the famous London square. Jet, Chuck, and Bruce were behind him, squeezed around a long tube that ran through the middle of the cabin, which sucked up trash into a large container at the back of the vehicle.

"This is an excellent disguise, Donnie," said Chuck.

"Actually it's a *rubbish* disguise," said Jet, with a chuckle.

Bruce pulled his head out of a take-out box and said, "Rubbish? It's the first one we've used that actually collects food—it's brilliant."

"I can't believe you're eating again," said Jet. "You ate twelve bags of jellied crickets on the plane here."

"That was just a snack. Look, I found half a burger," Bruce exclaimed, excitedly holding up the soggy specimen. He took a big bite. "Hmm, there's a bit too much ketchup, but it's nice of them to leave the pickle in."

"Bruce, you don't know where that's been," said Chuck, wrinkling his nose in disgust.

"Yeah, but I know where it's going," he replied, taking another huge bite.

Donnie pressed a button and the machine came to a standstill. "The meeting point is directly below us," he said. He pressed another button, which opened a hatch in the base of the vehicle, revealing a drain below. "This must be the way in."

"I wonder why Grandmaster One-Eye told us to come here. It's all very mysterious," said Jet.

"He said he received a message from an old friend," said Chuck. "And that it was a top secret mission."

"Hey, look! Street entertainers," said
Bruce, distracted by a man juggling with
flaming torches next to the vehicle.

"Fire juggling. Pah!" said Jet. "If I was a
street performer I'd demonstrate my new
move, the Quake Maker."

"What's that?" asked Bruce.

"I'll show you."

"Jet, no!" started Donnie. "Not inside the—"

It was too late. Jet leaped up and came crashing back down. Had they been outside, the force would have caused the ground to shake, knocking anyone nearby off their feet. But inside the street cleaner it had a different effect—the entire vehicle collapsed in a heap.

"Whoops! Sorry," said Jet.

"Bruce, Jet, Donnie," yelled Chuck. "Into the drain before anyone spots us!"

Donnie keyed a code into a tiny keypad on the drain cover and it slid open. One by one, each of the meerkats slipped through, sliding down a chute and dropping into the pitch-black drain below.

"Where are we?" asked Bruce. "I can't see a thing."

There was an electronic whirring as the drain cover slid back over the entry point. A light flickered on to reveal that they were in a room filled with technological gadgetry. The walls were lined with screens displaying CCTV footage from all around London. Sitting by a console covered in rows of buttons was a lumbering bulldog wearing a small bowler hat. He turned to face them, revealing that he had a monocle in his left eye and a scar down the right side of his face.

"Quite an entrance," he said. "It reminds me of the time I had to evacuate a tank after some fool pulled the pin out of a grenade, thinking he was opening a tin of sardines." He chuckled. "Clan of the Scorpion, thank you for responding to my request for assistance. Allow me to introduce myself. I'm Major Works, chief of the British Secret Secret Service."

GOFISH

Gareth P. Jones

What did you want to be when you grew up?
At various points, a writer, a musician, an intergalactic bounty hunter and, for a limited period, a graphic designer. (I didn't know what that meant, but I liked the way it sounded.)

When did you realize you wanted to be a writer?
I don't remember realizing it. I have always loved stories. From a very young age, I enjoyed making them up. As I'm not very good at making things up on the spot, this invariably involved having to write them down.

What's your most embarrassing childhood memory?
Seriously? There are too many. I have spent my entire life saying and doing embarrassing things. Just thinking about some of them is making me cringe. Luckily, I have a terrible memory, so I can't remember them all, but no, I'm not going to write any down for you. If I did that, I'd never be able to forget them.

What's your favorite childhood memory?
To be honest with you, I don't remember my childhood very well at all (I told you I had a bad memory), but I do recall how my dad used to tell me stories. He would make them up as he went along, most likely borrowing all sorts of elements from the books he was reading without me knowing.

As a young person, who did you look up to most?
My mom and dad, Prince, Michael Jackson, all of Monty Python, and Stephen Fry.

What was your favorite thing about school?
Laughing with my friends.

What was your least favorite thing about school?
I had a bit of a hard time when I moved from the Midlands to London at the age of twelve because I had a funny accent. But don't worry, it was all right in the end.

What were your hobbies as a kid? What are your hobbies now?
I love listening to and making music. My hobbies haven't really changed over the years, except that there's a longer list of instruments now. When I get a chance, I like idling away the day playing trumpet, guitar, banjo, ukulele, mandolin (and piano if there's one in the vicinity). I also like playing out with my friends.

What was your first job, and what was your "worst" job?

My first job was working as a waiter. That's probably my worst job, too. As my dad says, I was a remarkably grumpy waiter. I'm not big on all that serving-people malarkey.

What book is on your nightstand now?

I have a pile of books from my new publisher. I'm trying to get through them before I meet the authors. I'm half-way through *Maggot Moon* by Sally Gardner, which is written in the amazing voice of a dyslexic boy.

How did you celebrate publishing your first book?

The first time I saw one of my books in a shop, I was so excited that I caused something of a commotion. I managed to persuade an unsuspecting customer to buy it so I could sign it for her son.

Where do you write your books?

Anywhere and everywhere. Here are some of the locations I have written the Ninja Meerkats series: On the 185 and the 176 buses in London, various airplanes, Hong Kong, Melbourne, all over New Zealand, a number of cafes and bars between San Diego and San Francisco, New Quay in South Wales, and my kitchen.

What sparked your imagination for the Ninja Meerkats?

The idea came from the publishing house, but from the moment I heard it, I really wanted to write it. It reminded me of lots of action-packed cartoons I used to watch when I was young. I love the fact that I get to cram in lots of jokes and puns, fast action, and crazy outlandish plots.

The Ninja Meerkats are awesome fighters; have you ever studied martial arts? If so, what types?
Ha, no. If I was to get into a fight, my tactic would be to fall over and hope that whoever was attacking me lost interest.

If you were a Ninja Meerkat, what would your name be?
Hmm, how about Gareth *POW!* Jones?

What's your favorite exhibit or animal at the zoo?
Funnily enough, I like the meerkats. I was at a zoo watching them the other day when it started to rain. They suddenly ran for cover, looking exactly like their human visitors.

What's Bruce's favorite food?
Anything with the words ALL YOU CAN EAT written above it.

If you had a catchphrase like Bruce Force! or Ninja-Boom! what would it be?
That's a tricky one. How about PEN POWER!

If you were a Ninja Meerkat, what would your special ninja skill be?
I like to think I'd be like Jet, and always working on a new skill. When I got into school, I took the Random

Move Generator! We used it to come up with new moves, like the Floating Butterfly Punch and the Ultimate Lemon Punch.

What is your favorite thing about real-life meerkats? Have you ever met a meerkat?
I was lucky enough to go into a meerkat enclosure recently. They were crawling all over me, trying to get a good view. It was brilliant.

What challenges do you face in the writing process, and how do you overcome them?
The challenge with writing the Ninja Meerkats books is mostly about the plotting. It's trying to get all the twists and turns to work, and to avoid them feeling predictable. When I hit problems, I write down as many options as I can think of from the completely ordinary to utterly ridiculous. Once they're all down on paper, the right answer normally jumps out at me.

Which of your characters is most like you?
I'd like to say that I'm wise and noble like Chuck, but I'm probably more like the Ringmaster as we're both always coming up with new ways to take over the world.

What makes you laugh out loud?
My friends.

What do you do on a rainy day?
Play guitar, write, watch TV, or go out with my sword-handled umbrella.

What's your idea of fun?
Answering questionnaires about myself. Actually, to-morrow, I'm going to a music festival with my wife where we will dance and cavort. That should be fun.

What's your favorite song?
There are far too many to mention, but today I think I'll go for "Feel Good Inc." by Gorillaz.

Who is your favorite fictional character?
Another tricky one, but today I'll say Ged from the Earth-sea Trilogy by Ursula K. Le Guin.

What was your favorite book when you were a kid?
As a child, I especially loved *The Phantom Tollbooth* by Norton Juster.

What's your favorite TV show or movie?
Raiders of the Lost Ark.

If you were stranded on a desert island, who would you want for company?
My wife and son, then probably my friend Pete, as he's really handy and would be able to make and build things.

If you could travel anywhere in the world, where would you go and what would you do?
I'd like to go to Canada next. Ideally, I'd like to go and live there for a bit. I've never been to South America. There are also lots of parts of America I haven't visited yet.

SQUARE FISH

If you could travel in time, where would you go and what would you do?
I think I'd travel to the future and see what's changed and whether anyone's invented a new kind of umbrella.

What's the best advice you have ever received about writing?
Don't tell the story, show the story.

What advice do you wish someone had given you when you were younger?
Everything's probably going to be fine, so it's best to enjoy yourself.

Do you ever get writer's block? What do you do to get back on track?
It feels like tempting fate, but I don't really believe in writer's block. I think if you can't write, you're doing the wrong thing. You may need to plan or jot down options or go for a walk.

What do you want readers to remember about your books?
I'd settle for a general feeling of having enjoyed them.

What would you do if you ever stopped writing?
I'd do a full stop. If this is for an American audience, I guess that would be a period.

What should people know about you?
I'm a very silly man.

What do you like best about yourself?
I'm a very silly man.

Do you have any strange or funny habits? Did you when you were a kid?
I talk to myself a lot, which is probably pretty common, but the difference is that I don't listen to what I'm saying.